A FURL OF
FAIRY WIND

Other Books by Mollie Hunter

Mollie Hunter

A FURL OF FAIRY WIND

four stories

Drawings by Stephen Gammell

HARPER & ROW, PUBLISHERS

New York, Hagerstown, San Francisco, London

FIRST EDITION

Library of Congress Cataloging in Publication Data
McIlwraith, Maureen Mollie Hunter McVeigh, date
    A furl of fairy wind.

    SUMMARY: Four tales in which people encounter fairies
and brownies for the first time.
    1. Fairies—Juvenile fiction. [1. Fairies—Fiction]
I. Gammell, Stephen. II. Title.
PZ7.M18543Fu   398.2'1 [Fic]   76-58732
ISBN 0-06-022674-9
ISBN 0-06-022675-7 lib. bdg.

four stories

To Charlotte Z. with love—
and my thanks for
"a good morning's digging."

M.H.

A FURL OF FAIRY WIND

THE BROWNIE

There is nothing you can do if you have a Brownie in the house, except to leave him a bowl of hot porridge every night by the fire, with plenty of milk in it and a long-handled spoon to sup with.

This does not mean, of course, that a house would be better off without a Brownie in it, because—whatever he does by day—he will be awake most of the night, sweeping the hearth, washing up any dirty plates and dishes that have been left about, mending and polishing anything he can find to mend or polish. And all he asks in return is the bowl of hot porridge, to sleep by the kitchen fire when his work is finished—and to be left alone!

The Brownie that lived at Bilbeg Farm had come down from the hill one very cold winter's night when the grass was crackling with frost, and the sky was dark and low with the snow that would soon fall. The windows of the farmhouse were dark except for the small red glow of the fire banked on the kitchen hearth, and the door was locked, for the farmer and his wife had gone to bed. But you cannot keep a Brownie out with a locked door. And so the Brownie came in. He poked gently at the fire and stretched out his strong brown fingers to the blaze, and when he had stopped shivering he decided to stay at Bilbeg Farm.

The farmer's wife was an untidy woman, and when she came down in the morning to find her kitchen clean and tidy with a good fire blazing on the hearth, she knew there must be a Brownie in the house. She was careful not to mention this to her husband, however, in case he thought she was talking nonsense. All she did, in fact, before she went to bed the next night, was to leave out a bowlful of rich, salty porridge swimming with creamy milk and with a long-handled spoon stuck in it.

A poor housewife she might have been, but she was a grand cook, and when the Brownie had supped this porridge he was glad to do the work of the house in exchange. He even swept out the stable, groomed the horses, and polished their harness; all of which, as well as seeing the kitchen being kept neat as a new pin, was enough to surprise even the farmer into thinking there must be a Brownie in the house. And so, without the farmer or his wife ever mentioning their thoughts on this to one another, everything went along very happily at Bilbeg Farm.

A while went by like this, with matters running so smoothly that the farmer began to grow rich. Bilbeg seemed small to him then, and so he decided to leave it and buy a much larger farm that he had had his eye on for a long time.

"Don't tempt your luck," said his wife, thinking of the Brownie.

The farmer laughed. "My luck will go with me," said he, also thinking of the Brownie and feeling sure it would move with them when it knew what a fine house they were going to. His wife, however, was a bit wiser than this. She knew that once a Brownie has chosen a house to stay in, it will not leave it for another; and so, it was with a heavy heart that she prepared to leave Bilbeg.

The day that she did so was also the day that she met for the first time with the wife of the new farmer. It would be just as well, she thought, to warn this woman about the Brownie, and so she told all about him and how he was paid for his work. The Brownie heard her at this, of course, and came in as usual for his porridge that night; but the new farmer's wife was a city-bred woman with a diploma in household management and she needed no Brownie to do her work for her. But in any case, she had decided, there was no such thing as a Brownie. Everything the old farmer's wife had told her had been a lot of nonsense, and so there was no bowl of porridge there that night.

Beside the cold ashes on the kitchen hearth, the Brownie danced with rage and beat his head with his clenched fists till it ached. Then he seized the poker and scattered the ashes of the fire all over the room. Running outside to the stable, he pulled all the harness off the walls and slashed at it with a carving knife till the leather hung in ribbons. Then he tramped back into the house and made muddy footprints all over the floor as he pulled cups and plates from their places and sent them crashing from one end of the room to the other.

The farmer and his wife thought they had taken leave of their senses when they saw the mess the next morning. The farmer examined all the doors and windows, but they were locked and fastened as he had left them the night before. His wife watched him harness up the trap with ropes in place of the leather harness that had been slashed, and as he rode off in this to fetch a policeman, she wondered if she should mention the Brownie.

She was afraid of being laughed at, however, and all the time the policeman was asking questions and measuring things, she never

said a word. When she went to bed that night, she was still thinking about the Brownie and wondering if it would do yet more damage; and sure enough, the next morning the place looked as if a storm had struck it. Off went the farmer to fetch the policeman again, but this time he gave his wife a very strange look before he left.

That look puzzled her until she realized it meant he was wondering if *she* had done the damage, because there had been no one in the house but themselves, and all the doors and windows had been locked as before. The policeman came and went without finding out any more than he had the first time, and the farmer's wife made up her mind. She waited till her husband was asleep, and then went quietly down the stairs to the kitchen.

Outside the kitchen door she stopped and listened. There was a banging and thumping noise coming from inside, and she stood with her hand on the door latch, afraid to go any further in case she met the Brownie. The banging stopped, and after there had been quiet for a while she pushed open the door and stepped into the kitchen. There was nobody to be seen there, but the furniture was all overturned, with books, cushions, and other things strewn all over the room.

The place was really in a terrible mess, but without stopping to look at the damage to it, the farmer's wife went quickly up to the pot rack, took down a pot, and ran water into it. Then she fetched the meal jar and measured meal from it into a cup. She put salt in the water, and when the water had come to a boil, she stirred the meal slowly into it, moving the pot to the hob and spooning out the lumps as the porridge simmered up to a boil again. And all the time she was doing this, she could hear somebody breathing.

The nearer the porridge came to being ready, the nearer the breathing came to her. She never looked up once, all the same, and when the porridge was ready she poured it into a bowl, tipped in a jugful of milk from that morning's milking, and set the bowl down on the hearth with a long-handled spoon sticking out of it. Then she went out of the kitchen, waited again outside the door, and again she listened. The sound of someone supping porridge came to her, and as soon as she heard this, she hurried back to bed.

When the Brownie had finished supping the porridge, he put down the bowl and looked all around the room. Then he started to work. He cleaned out the fireplace, laid and lit the fire, and when it was crackling merrily up the chimney, he swept up the broken crockery, put the furniture back into place, stitched up the torn curtains and cushions, polished the floor, and mended the harness.

There was so much damage to be repaired, in fact, that he had to work steadily at these and other jobs until the dawn, with never a minute to doze off beside the fire as he would have liked to do.

When the farmer came downstairs at four o'clock to milk the cows, he looked into the kitchen to see what further damage had been done in the night, and just about died of amazement at the neatness and shining brightness of everything there. When he got over the shock of this, he ran upstairs shouting to his wife to come and look. Then he rushed out to the stable to see what had happened there.

The harness was back on the walls, neatly mended. The brasses were polished, and the horses were groomed. His wife came running out as he stood staring at all this. She, too, stared around the stable, and then she began to laugh.

When she had finished laughing, she told her husband about the Brownie, but he didn't believe her.

"There's no such thing!" he exclaimed.

In the hayloft above their heads, the Brownie sat up on his elbow and grunted angrily.

"Hush!" said the farmer's wife. "I think he can hear you."

Away she went out of the stable then, with the farmer following her and wondering still what they could do about all the strange things that had happened. The Brownie settled down in the warm hay and went to sleep again, for he knew very well that there is nothing you *can* do if you have a Brownie in the house, except to leave him a bowl of hot porridge every night by the fire, with plenty of milk in it and a long-handled spoon to sup with.

THE ENCHANTED BOY

There was once a boy who went into the forest on Midsummer's Eve.

This was a foolish thing to do because the People who live in the forest belong to the fairy world, and Midsummer's Eve for these People is the magic night of all the year, so that they do not like to have strangers among them then.

The boy's grandmother, who was a very old and very wise woman, warned him not to go into the forest.

"No good can come of it," said she. But the boy was curious about the People and would not listen to her.

The forest was big, and old, and dark. The trees in it were tall, with great thick branches that shut the boy off from the moon and the stars, but he managed to find a path and this path took him to the center of the forest.

There was a great stillness in that place. The leaves of the trees made no rustle or movement. There was no stir or whisper from the grass. The boy stood listening to this stillness and wondering at it, but he was not afraid. He called aloud a certain name he had heard in stories quietly told, and which is the true name of the People who live in the forest; but that was also a foolish thing to do because the thing these People like least of all is to have their true name cried out like this.

On the instant the sound of it was uttered, they were all around him. The boy had no warning of their coming, no chance to run from the danger he could now sense from them. They were simply there, in no more than the time it took for him to draw a breath; and he knew this was so, even although the forest was still dark and they, themselves, were invisible. He could hear them as well as feel their presence; and at this, he became very much afraid.

They crowded close to him and cried out angrily. They poked their sharp fingers into his flesh. They pushed him this way and that. And the noise of all this was like the wild shrieking of many birds. The feel of it was like sharp claws digging into him and the wings of birds beating all around.

The boy could no more save himself from them than a leaf could save itself from being tossed in a storm. But suddenly a great light shone, and all was still again. The boy looked into the light. The People had become visible in the moment of its shining, and he saw then how beautiful they were, and in their anger, how terrible.

Their Queen stood among them dressed in robes of green silk. There was a belt of gold around her waist and a golden crown on her head. Long hair of palest gold flowed down her back, and it was from her that the light came. The boy looked at her face, and it was so beautiful that a great longing came over him to be always with her.

A vision of the world where she was Queen grew in his mind with the look she gave him, and this world was a perfect one. The colors of it were rainbow-bright, every face in it was a fair one, and the sounds that rang through it were like all the music he had ever tried to remember. But this music in the boy's vision was the voice

of the Queen speaking a spell that enchanted him, and the moment this spell was uttered, his longing became so great that it was like a pain in his heart.

In that moment also, the Queen and her People vanished, and everything was dark again. The boy stood there, dazzled by darkness and aching with longing. Then, sadly, he set his foot to the path home, looking backwards over his shoulder all the time he walked; for this was the spell the Queen had put on him—that he should always be looking back into the past, and longing for what he had once seen there.

The boy's grandmother was kneeling to light the fire when he came into the house again, and one look at him was enough to let her see that he was under a spell. Tears of pity for this ran like rain down her face then, but the boy said nothing to her. He seated himself by the fire, not even speaking a word of regret for his foolishness, and at this, the grandmother became angry.

"I warned you," she scolded, "but you paid me no heed. And now what is to become of you?"

Still the boy said nothing, but only looked back over his shoulder at the past. The grandmother wept again, for pity of herself this time, as well as for him.

"What will become of *us*?" she cried. "There is no one will take an enchanted boy for an apprentice, and what will we do if you cannot work?"

The boy was still too wrapped in his own thoughts to trouble with these questions.

"Grandmother," said he, "don't weep, but listen to me. When I look back over my shoulder like this it seems to me that I am looking into the past, and I can see further back there than last night, or last month, or last year. I can even see back to the time when I was very small and my father and mother were alive."

"A big handsome man your father was," the grandmother sighed, "with black hair and a fine, strong face. And your mother had hair that was red-gold and shining as a new penny."

"Yes," said the boy, "the same color as your hair was, grandmother, when you were a girl. I can see that as well when I look into the past. And further back yet I can see, right back to a time when it seems the world must have been new, with all the colors in it bright, and all the people beautiful. But why should it be so with me, grandmother? And why should I have a terrible longing to be part of that long-ago world?"

Tears came to the boy's eyes as he asked these questions, and the grandmother wept with him.

"It's because of Them and the spell They put on you," she told him. "That world so far in the past is Their world the way you must have glimpsed it when they enchanted you, and the spell on you now means that you will be forever looking and longing for it."

The boy felt the pain of his longing become even greater at this, yet still he could not believe he would never find that world again. He rose from the fire and wandered away from the house, looking backwards, always looking backwards, with the pain he felt showing in his eyes. And so he was for a year and a day from that time, a wandering creature always looking and longing but never finding what he sought.

At the end of this year and a day, the grandmother had word that an old beggarwoman had come to the village and that she had charms and medicines to sell. The grandmother sent for her, thinking she might have something that would cure the boy, and the beggarwoman came to the house.

The grandmother looked at her and saw only an old woman dressed in rags, but when the boy looked at her he saw the Queen of the People who live in the forest. The Queen put her hand into the leather bag that was hung about her waist, and from this bag she took a coin.

The coin was large, and red-gold in color. She spun it into the air, where it glowed and flashed with all the colors of the rainbow; and as it spun, it gave out a sound that was like small silver bells ringing faint and very far away.

The Queen caught the coin as it fell. She held it out to the boy and told him, "Spin this, as I have done. Then you will have no

more remembrance of me or my People, and you will no longer walk looking backwards into the past."

The boy wanted to be healed of the spell on him, yet he did not want to give up his vision of the world he had such a longing to find; and so he hesitated. Then the thought of spinning the coin became too much for him. He could not resist taking it from the Queen, and as he flicked it into the air, she cried, "The spell is lifted—but let this much of the wonders it showed you, be yours forever!"

The coin spun through the air, tumbling and turning like a little world of colors bright as the first light of creation, ringing with music as sweet and faraway as the music of dreams; and before it had come to rest again, the beggarwoman who was the Queen had vanished.

28

The boy clasped the coin in his hand and smiled to think it was his own. Once more he spun it, thinking as he did so that the kind of world it made was beautiful as the perfect one he seemed to have heard about sometime, somewhere; but he was healed of the spell on him, so that he could not recall when or where this had been. Nor had he any memory at all of how he had come to possess such a marvel; and the grandmother—being a very wise woman —did not tell him.

HI JOHNNY

Hi Johnny was a peddler.

All day he tramped along country roads with a pack on his back, and in this pack he carried goods to sell to farmers' wives—things like pins, needles, knives, and scissors, and very often pots and pans as well. Hi Johnny also had a strong, knobbly stick to help him on his way, and since this was usually a lonely one, he was always eager to stop and talk to anyone he met.

"Hi! Hi!" he would shout, waving his stick until he was near enough to pass the time of day in a quieter manner. This made

31

people laugh, so that he was always welcome among them, and it was for this that he had come to be called Hi Johnny.

There was one summer's day, however, when someone saw Hi Johnny before he saw them. He was tramping that day along a road that ran through hill country. This road was deserted, except for himself, yet suddenly he heard a voice call, "Hi Johnny!"

The voice was a woman's, and he looked around in amazement at the sound of it, because the road was still empty so far as he knew and there was no house within miles of that place. Right behind him, all the same, he saw the woman who had called him.

She was dressed in a green cloak that covered her to the ankles. A green hood was pulled down over her hair, which was white like that of an old woman. Yet still Hi Johnny could not tell whether she was young or old because her face had no wrinkles and her eyes were as bright and clear as those of a girl.

"You've sprung up sudden, ma'am," said he, staring at her, and the woman smiled at this.

"I'm always where there are eyes to see me," she told him.

Hi Johnny thought this was an odd answer to give; and when he looked again at her old/young face he decided there was something altogether odd about her, but he got ready to do business with her all the same.

"Was it something from my pack you wanted?" he asked.

And the woman told him, "It could be, because what I want to buy is an iron pot."

"Then," said Hi Johnny, slinging off his pack and reaching into it, "you've come to the right man, because I have one here that will last you a lifetime."

"Aye, that looks a good pot," said she, taking a long look at the one Hi Johnny handed to her. Then she added, "I'll buy it from you," and putting her hand into the pouch at her girdle she took out a gold coin.

"Wait now," said Hi Johnny, eyeing the gold. "I'm only a poor peddler. I don't carry change for that kind of money."

"Ah well," said the woman, "that's my misfortune. You take the gold piece, I'll take the pot, and we'll call it a bargain."

Hi Johnny stood there with the gold piece in his hand, thinking hard. In his thirty years of traveling country roads, he had heard many a strange tale; and strangest of all were those tales that spoke of the fairy people who had plenty of gold, *but no iron*. Also, he had heard, they always wore green and covered their heads with green hoods. What was more, they could change their appearance at will, and come and go so suddenly that no man could see how they came or where they went. And now, here was this woman with her young face and white hair covered by a green hood, suddenly appearing and offering him as much gold for one iron pot as would buy her twenty of the same!

"I'll find out who she is," he said to himself, "if it kills me! And besides, I might make a lot more than one gold piece out of it." And to the woman he said, "Maybe I could walk the way you mean to go, ma'am, for I've a notion that this gold coin you gave me might be my luck-piece."

The woman gave him a long look. "Do you know who I am?" she asked.

"No. But—" said Hi Johnny cautiously, "I think I can guess."

The woman smiled at this, a rather strange little smile. "And you're not afraid?" she asked.

Hi Johnny shook his head, even although he had felt a touch of fear at the strangeness of her smile.

"Come with me then," she told him, "and if it's true you are not afraid, that coin might indeed be your luck-piece."

Hi Johnny picked up his pack, ready to go up or down the road as she chose, but the woman left the road altogether and struck off into the hills instead. Hi Johnny followed; and although there was no path that he could see, she never faltered, but kept walking swiftly until they were deep in the hills and there was nothing to be seen around them but grass and streams and heather.

There was nothing to be heard either except the burble of the streams and the sad cries of curlews wheeling over the hillside, because the woman spoke no word in all the miles they walked

together, and Hi Johnny could tell from her looks that his own talk would not be welcome.

It was not until dusk was falling that the woman stopped at last among some grassy hillocks covered with tall green bracken. She parted the fronds of bracken on one of these mounds; and behind the fronds, Hi Johnny saw, there was a green door. It swung open to her touch, and bending low, she went inside. With a fearful heart, but feeling he had come too far to go back now, Hi Johnny followed her.

Along a dark passage that sloped downwards, she led him, and at the end of it he stood blinking in astonishment, for this passage opened out into a great hall lit by hundreds of candles and full of people. They were a good bit smaller than himself, these people, but their faces had a strange, flower-like beauty. Their bodies were slender and very graceful, and all of them were dressed in green with green hoods on their heads. They were also, all of them, as active as bees in a hive.

Some were busily shaping and polishing tiny, sharp arrowheads. Some of them worked with metal at a furnace, some were weaving on looms that held webs of fine, green material. Those who were not at work of one kind or another were dancing to the music of reed pipes played by others of their number, and wherever Hi Johnny looked among all this activity, he saw the glitter of gold.

The looms of the weavers had golden frames. The metal being worked at the furnace was gold. The hundreds of candles were set in golden candle-holders, and all the men as well as all the women there wore bracelets and necklaces of gold made in strange and wonderful designs.

Hi Johnny stood quite entranced by this first sight of the fairy people—because that was what they were, of course, and he realized this instantly. But it was still their gold, more than anything else, that enchanted him so that he could not take his eyes off it.

"Will you *look* at that!" he breathed, turning at last to the old woman who had brought him there. But she had gone, and in her place stood another of the fairy people, the most beautiful creature he had ever seen, with a golden crown on her head, her green dress fastened by a golden girdle, and a white rod in her hand.

She smiled at him and said, "Now, Hi Johnny, let us see if the golden coin was your luck-piece."

Here was another wonder, thought Hi Johnny, because these words told him that this fairy queen and the old woman of the roads were one and the same person; and while he was still in confusion over this, she took him by the hand and led him to the center of the great hall.

The fairy people crowded around him, talking among themselves in sweet, thin voices, but with many a laugh in Hi Johnny's direction. Hi Johnny swung his pack off his back and stood there, feeling very big and clumsy and foolish beside all these clever, graceful little creatures. But when he opened his pack and they saw what was inside it, all this was changed, and it was Hi Johnny then who was lord of the fairies' hall.

Scissors, pins, knives, pots, needles—all the things made of iron or steel were snatched up by the fairy people, and in exchange for them, they thrust gold on Hi Johnny—gold in every shape and form, from the raw metal straight out of the earth to the most delicate of ornaments.

By the time his pack was empty, Hi Johnny was a rich man. The fairies brought him heather-ale, the drink that only they knew the secret of brewing. They pressed him to drink of it, and by the time he had tasted this and thought on the long walk back across the hills in darkness, he needed small urging to spend the rest of the night with them. Also, he wanted to celebrate his new fortune; and so, when the moon came up, they all went aboveground and danced wild dances in a ring, Hi Johnny leaping as nimbly as the rest, snapping his fingers and kicking up his heels with a fine flourish.

Between dances, too, when he flung himself down on the grass to draw breath again, he fell to dreaming of what he would do with his riches. No more "Hi Johnny" and tramping the roads in wet or shine for him. He would be "Lord Johnny" and live in a mansion house, with servants and fine horses and hounds with scarlet

leashes around their necks. And so, with heather-ale, dancing, and dreams of gold, Hi Johnny passed his night among the fairies.

When the first red ray of the sun slanted over the hills to the east, Hi Johnny picked up his heavy packful of gold and his knobbly stick. He looked around to say good-bye to the fairy people, but they had all vanished underground—all except the woman he had met on the road, the old woman with the young face. Hi Johnny took off his bonnet and bent his knee to her, for he knew his manners to a queen.

"I thank you for your kindness, Ma'am," said he, "and although there's no longer any need for me to travel the roads with a pack on my back, I'll come and visit your people again one day, if I may."

The queen's face was stern. "No, Hi Johnny," she told him. "You may *not* come back here."

Hi Johnny looked up at her, astonished. "I've done nothing wrong, Ma'am," he protested. "Was I not honest in my dealings with you!"

"You were," the queen agreed, "but that was when you were a poor peddler; and since then, you have become a rich man. In your head you have the dream of living the life of a lord; but rich men always want to be still richer than they are. And in your heart, Hi Johnny, you know that you mean to come back with goods not half so worthy as those you sold to us, and to get as much gold again for them."

Hi Johnny hung his head in shame, for she had indeed seen into his heart.

"Ma'am," he said, "you speak no more than the truth." And suddenly then it came to him that he would have little use for life in a fine mansion if he could not be traveling the lonely roads, the friend and welcome guest of every person he met. He remembered the scream of a hare he had seen killed by hounds, and thought it would be a cruel thing to keep hounds in scarlet leashes to kill the gentle hares. And could he never taste the heather-ale again and dance wildly with the fairies under the moon to the music of reed pipes, he knew his life would be bitter to its end.

"Hang all riches!" Hi Johnny shouted, and tearing open his pack he tipped the whole of its golden contents onto the grass. From among this pile he chose a few small pieces of gold which he judged would cover the value of the goods he had sold the fairy people. Then, with a grin on his face, he looked up at the fairy woman and told her, "Now I am paid justly."

She smiled at him. "Your way lies over there," said she, pointing to the east. "But come back to see us, Hi Johnny, for now you are welcome to do that."

"Thank you, Ma'am. That's all I wanted to hear," he told her, and slipping the gold into his pocket, he moved away in the direction she had pointed.

"Hi Johnny!" she called after him. He stopped, looking over his shoulder, and saw her standing in her green gown with the great heap of gold glittering at her feet.

"You are taking better than gold with you," she called. "You have found the secret of happiness."

"I believe I have, Ma'am," he shouted back to her. "I do believe I have!"

And he trudged off towards the rising sun with his empty pack on his back, swinging his great knobbly stick and whistling merrily.

A FURL OF FAIRY WIND

There was once a girl who never smiled. Her name was Margaret, and she was a plain girl—or at least, she looked plain. She was also lonely, with no family of her own, and she never smiled because she had forgotten how to smile.

The old woman who looked after Margaret was rather a strange person, always telling stories about ghosts and witches and fairies and other mysterious creatures, and Margaret was never sure whether or not she should believe these stories. The old woman, however, was wiser than she seemed to be.

"Some day," said she, "you will hear a furl of fairy wind, and then you will know that all I have told you is true. Furthermore, something good will happen to you on that day. And then also, you will find you can remember how to smile."

Now the old woman had already told Margaret plenty about fairies. Margaret also knew that a furl of wind is one that goes round and round like a whirlwind. Yet still the old woman's words made no sense to her, and so this was something else she could not believe.

It was not long after this, however, that the old woman had a visit from someone who was looking for a servant-maid. This visitor was a young woman, who said, "I have a young baby in the house, and a baby makes a lot of extra work. I need a strong girl to help me with that, and I was told you have such a girl here."

"I've only got Margaret," the old woman told her, "and she's young yet to be a servant-maid. But you can take her if you like, and she'll soon learn how to look after a baby."

Margaret did not mind being sent off like this, because taking care of a baby sounded like pleasant work. She even began to wonder if it might turn out to be the good thing the old woman had said would happen to her, but when she reached the young woman's house, she was sorely disappointed.

The baby was a boy—a fine, strong boy, who kicked and laughed and slept soundly and took his milk the way a healthy baby should, but the mother would not trust him to anyone except herself. Instead of helping to care for him, Margaret found she was only allowed to scrub and polish and do kitchen work. The mother was kind to her, certainly, but only with the sort of kindness given to a stranger, so that still she could not remember how to smile and went about her work looking as plain as ever.

Margaret had only been a few weeks in this house, however, when something terrible happened. She was standing at the kitchen sink one day, peeling vegetables with a sharp little iron knife she kept for that purpose. The mother was upstairs making beds. The baby was lying in its cot in the room next to the kitchen, and suddenly from this room there came a great cry of fright.

Now Margaret had grown very fond of this baby, even although she was never allowed to touch it. Straight away, without even bothering to put down her knife, she rushed into the next room and up to the baby's cot. She bent down to look inside the cot, but there was no pink, fat, smiling baby there. What she saw looking up at her instead was a little, thin baby, with a face as brown and wrinkled as a dried-up nut, and the wickedest grin on it you could imagine.

In a flash then, Margaret remembered a story the old woman had once told about a creature she called a changeling. . . .

Sometimes the fairies will make a change between a human baby and one of their own kind, and this changeling lies in the cot while they steal the human baby away to their own land. But they know that the human baby will need its mother to look after it until it can grow up to be their servant in that land; and so they steal the baby's mother as well, and carry the two of them off in a furl of fairy wind. But iron is the most powerful of all charms against fairy magic, and if only someone can be brave enough—

Margaret looked down at the little iron knife in her hand. She could hear the furl of fairy wind now, blowing all around the house, and so she knew there was no time to lose. The changeling saw her look at the knife, and its wicked little face twisted with anger.

"Don't you dare!" it screamed, but Margaret was already halfway to the door.

She ran from the house, still hearing the furl of fairy wind wildly blowing, and the moment she was outside, she saw the great whirling cloud of dust it had sucked up from the ground. The wind caught her hair, blowing it straight up from her head, and she was frightened by this—but not too frightened to remember the rest of the old woman's story and to know from this that there was only one thing she could do now to save the mother and her baby.

"This is mine!" she shouted. *"That is yours!"* And with these words, she threw the iron knife straight up into the dust-cloud at the heart of the furl of fairy wind.

A screech of many voices answered Margaret's shout, a screech so high and thin and wild that it hurt her ears. The whirling wind stopped on the instant of its sound, the knife fell back to earth. And there before her stood the mother—looking very pale and shaken, it's true, but quite unhurt, and with the baby clutched safely in her arms.

Margaret took one look to make sure they were both unharmed, then she ran back to the house to gaze down into the cot; but the changeling had vanished at the same time as the wind had stopped, and the cot was empty. In came the mother then, babbling her thanks at every step, and telling Margaret that she would no longer be treated like a servant but like her own daughter.

"And to prove that," said she, putting the baby into Margaret's arms, "here is the boy to be a brother to you now, and for you to look after the way a sister should."

All of a sudden then, Margaret found she could remember how to smile—because this, at last, was the good thing that was to happen to her; to be one of a family again, with a mother and a young brother of her own. She was no longer plain, either, with this smile on her face. She was bonny, in fact—a really bonny girl; and the mother wondered at this.

"I thought you were plain," said she, "but I see now how wrong I was!"

Margaret had begun rocking the new brother in her arms, and she felt the smile tingling all over her face as she looked from him to the new mother. She said nothing, but she thought of the old woman telling her, *"Some day you will hear a furl of fairy wind . . ."*

And all by herself at that moment, in the house where Margaret used to live with her, the old woman also smiled.